Robots in Love

by

Rhys Hughes

Robots in Love
by Rhys Hughes

ISBN: 978-1-913766-35-1

Publication Date: 2025

www.eibonvalepress.co.uk

Contents

Robots in Love

or

Daftness and Chlorine:
an Interstellar Pastoral Romance

This work is a science fiction retelling of the ancient classical story of Daphnis and Chloe with robots and androids rather than goats and sheep, set on the asteroid L35B05 instead of Lesbos island, featuring space pirates, vacuum gods, escape pods, comets, nebulae and titanium rods, and a few nods to the tradition of nonsense verse. It could be worse than it actually is, so now polish your electric eyes for the coming rhythmic ride. Ready? Let's set off...

Prologue

While visiting the asteroid L35B05 I saw, in a museum set up for the education of human beings, an artificial crystal of great beauty. It was tetrahedral in shape and each glowing side projected a hologram full of quaint images of those odd beings that had dwelled in this asteroid a very long time ago. After gazing at the output of all four facets with wonder and admiration, I was filled with an urge to write a verbal equivalent to this crystal.

I fetched the curator in order that he might explain the moving pictures to me and thus learned that by viewing the outputs in the correct sequence, a story was presented in its entirety that was actually coherent on its own terms. I now take the opportunity to dedicate my work to Evolution and Mutation. For no one has escaped natural selection altogether, and no one ever can, but as for myself I hope the effort will not impair my genes.

Facet One

There is in the interior of this asteroid a large and impressive port facility where all manner of technical and business activities take place. Not more than a few dozen splorks from the port was a zone where a rich mining company had its centre of operations. Wandering the perimeter of this private area, the security guard Lam found a new robot being tended by an octopoid worker. The alien was rocking the young robot in its tentacles.

Lam's first plan was to ignore the scene but then he felt ashamed to show less empathy than an octopoid, so he waited until his shift was over and then took the tiny droid back to his apartment and to Myr, his legal mate, who at first was astonished at the idea of octopoids having robot babies, until he suggested that probably it had been abandoned by its true owners. They agreed to adopt it and gave it the arbitrary name of Daftness.

Two grobbles went by and a security guard in an adjacent zone where a company that specialised in chemical engineering was based found something similar. There was a niche cut into the interior wall of the hollow asteroid at this point where a shrine to Entropy had been set up and the guard, who was called Yas, noticed that one of the insectoid workers kept going into the niche. Curious to see what the alien was up to, Yas went into the niche too and found it caring for a baby android, rocking it in its feelers.

Just as Lam had done previously, Yas decided to take care of the foundling and carried it back to his own mate, Nubu, who thought the idea of adopting it was an excellent one. Because of its chemical composition they gave it the name of Chlorine. Nubu turned out to be an excellent carer, for she disliked the notion that an insectoid might be better in this regard than she was, and so she was keen to prove both her efficiency and dedication.

The robot and the android grew rapidly, the former metallic and beeping a lot, the latter plastic and more human in its vocalisations. Daftness grew through a process of stretching the compressed plates that formed his shell and

Chlorine grew by absorbing molecules from the surrounding air and incorporating them into her structure. Although artificial people had no objective gender back then, for the sake of this story Daftness was male and Chlorine female, and that is how they appeared to everyone who met them.

Daftness was now twenty grobbles old and Chlorine was two grobbles less than that, when Lam and Yas both had the same strange dream. Human beings often saw pictures in their heads at night without specifically requesting them. A very bizarre species indeed! But anyway, in this shared dream Lam and Yas saw Daftness and Chlorine standing at the mouth of a black hole and out of the black hole came a vast vacuum god with a quiver full of arrows that were spaghettified spaceships and a bow like a bent lightbeam.

This god lightly touched Daftness and then Chlorine and told them that the robot was destined to work as a security guard for mines and the android as a security guard for chemical plants. Lam and Yas were quite disappointed by this decision because they wanted their adopted beings to do something superior to their own professions, maybe an artistic occupation, creating ceramics or the composing of music or the writing of verse, something along those aesthetic lines.

But they were reluctant to oppose the will of a vacuum god and so they each taught their charges what they knew.

Lam instructed Daftness on how to stroll around a perimeter fence with protruding lips and a frown and how to wipe mining dust off himself, while at the same time Yas showed Chlorine the best way to saunter around the outside of an exclusion zone with jutting chin and a snarl and how to protect oneself from corrosive aerosols in the immediate environment. Both were fast learners and soon became accomplished sentries.

It was the beginning of the cosmic season of the binary star spring and the pulsar chorus was especially intense in the early hours and everyone who lived and worked on asteroid L35B05 was full of energy and enthusiasm. The mining company expanded the size of the work area and so did the chemical plant and soon the two industrial concerns were overlapping, which means that Daftness and Chlorine frequently passed each other in a convoluted loop as they walked their rounds, like two rogue moons influenced by the gravity of gas giants in an eccentric solar system. Daftness clanked and beeped, Chlorine squelched and susurrated, and all was exceedingly nice.

They became acquaintances and then friends and before long they would stop to chat about all sorts of topics, such as supernovae and tungsten junctions and binary finery. Daftness began to regard Chlorine as the most charming of all susurrating squelchers, and she thought of him as her personal clanking beeper. Sometimes they would take over each other's chores, Daftness resting under a quantum tree while Chlorine walked his route as well as her own, or Chlorine levitating cross-legged on a fountain of liquid helium while Daftness traced the double circumference of their working day.

Their amusements were innocent and callow (but only if those two words aren't synonyms) and are sure to raise a smile on the face of experienced entities (if those entities have faces). Chlorine would run to the element fields to pick titanium rods with which she wove baskets to carry demonstration models of electrons, mesons and quarks. Daftness would hop up and down on one leg and rotate his head at maximum speed while playing a fugue with his beep organs. Once he hopped so high on his ultra-highly-sprung leg that he bashed and dented his superconducting noggin on the rocky ceiling of the asteroid's interior and he had to have it straightened out by a specialist.

While they were engaged in those kinds of amusements, the vacuum god with the quiver contrived an interruption of a serious nature. A drogulus from another dimension had appeared and carried off one of the octopoid miners. The grim owners of the mine set electromagnetic traps for the drogulus but completely failed to capture it. They did, however, end up slaying many other unfortunate octopoids, who wandered into these traps, and nearly ended the existence of Daftness. This is roughly how it happened.

Two octopoids of rival spiritual clans were engaged in a fight. The combat became more violent until one of the contestants had an entire tentacle torn off and it scuttled away in fright. The victor slithered in close pursuit and Daftness pursued the pursuer. All three of them plunged headlong into a trap and soon they were crackling with energy and grimacing involuntarily and dancing like a trio of centrifugal loons and essentially not enjoying themselves at all. Luckily, Chlorine had witnessed the accident with her telescopic eyes and rushing to the rim of the forcefield and seeing Daftness was still alive she weakened the trap enough for him to escape by thrusting her tongue into the energy pulsation. Magnetism flowed into her throat and she swallowed it.

Daftness was fascinated by this action of hers and although he was sizzling and still shedding sparks, he looked up at her with an expression of awe on his alloyed face. She smiled back, plastic and fantastic, and they went together to a safe place, an abandoned canteen for spacecraft pilots that had failed years ago when the bottom fell out of the Boolean bagel market. Here he brushed himself down and polished his scorched body.

It occurs to me that I haven't properly described either of our two heroes in any detail, so allow me to do so belatedly. Daftness was approximately half a metre high, striped with bands of gold, silver, platinum, copper, osmium, zinc, iridium, titanium, tungsten and technetium, with powerful spring-loaded legs, a dodecahedral head, two mouths (one of them superfluous because they acted in sync), four extendable arms and a penchant for wiggling his ears that were large and hyperbolic and capable of receiving and sending transmissions from distant constellations, if one was willing to wait.

Chlorine was almost five metres tall, shaped like a human woman who is disguised as a prehistoric gorilla who desperately wants to be a cave bear. She had two shapely legs, a ceramic waist, carbon fibre hips, very broad shoulders, only two arms but ten fingers on each hand and twenty toes on each foot. Her own ears were small and radioactive. Her eyebrows were induction loops that enabled her to transfer electric charge from one unit to another, I am not sure exactly how. She had chips on her shoulder that acted like backup brains and she was very good at calculus and geometry.

While Daftness was grooming himself, Chlorine found herself gazing at his form with admiration and wonder. Never had she seen such a beautiful robot! He was now gleaming and the glow of remote quasars seemed to shine deep within his complex carapace. She felt an urge to stroke him but she resisted it, confused and slightly worried. This was the beginning of love or the cybernetic equivalent of love, algorithmic amour perhaps we ought to term it, and never again would she regard Daftness in the same way as before. As for the robot, he was logically aware of her attention and interest and it thrilled him in a way he was unable to teleologically define. He felt very strange.

One of the owners of the mining concern was a cyborg named Dorc with a human head and torso of an ore crusher and, unbeknownst to our two lovers, he had been quietly observing Chlorine for many weeks. Feeling his passion on the increase he started to despise Daftness and resolved that he would win the heart of Chlorine one way or another, even though she had no heart

His first notion was to give gifts to both of them to prove his friendship. He gave Daftness some chubbles from the planet Oriox and presented Chlorine with a bouquet of yiban gurkles from Rumple. Having thus insinuated himself into their fond regard, he by degrees neglected Daftness but every day brought something to Chlorine, a slab of plutonium fudge or a spintronic duckling. Innocent as she was, she liked to pass these presents on to Daftness, delighted at the opportunity to please him. Dorc decided now to change his tactics.

He appeared one morning and told them that it was a new company policy for all security guards and their employers to submit to a beauty competition. He humbly requested that Chlorine would act as an umpire. She agreed because she thought it was nothing more than a game. Then Dorc made the following strong speech as part of the impromptu contest:

"Dear Miss Android, please look at me. I am taller than Daftness and much stronger. My grinders can triturate the shells of spent nuclear reactors in a trice. I am successful and relatively wealthy, certainly rich enough to buy a comet if my tastes should ever become tantalised by whizzing balls of cosmic ice. I know at least nine thousand equations despite the fact I have an organic brain. I can beat my chest in unorthodox rhythms and if I concentrate hard enough my kneecaps will rotate at an extremely high velocity."

Chlorine clapped her hands to show her appreciation of his qualities but it was now the turn of Daftness to present his case. He said, "All that Dorc states is technically true, but consider how my lack of height has certain advantages. I can climb into smaller holes than he can and sit inside them for days. Although my physical strength is less than five percent of his, I can hop up and down and whistle and hum two different tunes at the same time. Making cheese from crude oil is something I am able to do. I am poor, yes, but so are vast hydrogen clouds and yet we gasp at their gorgeousness. I know twenty million equations and not only do my kneecaps rotate but so do my nipples. I can also communicate with pulsars and thumb my nose at satellites."

Chlorine could restrain herself no longer, but sprang forward and toppled Daftness over. Then she fell on top of him and rubbed herself all over his body and she marvelled at this reflexive reaction, which to her was baffling and even insane. Dorc stamped off in disgust, vowing to win Chlorine by an alternative method. Meanwhile, Daftness began to overheat and his beeping became atonal and ultrasonic. Chlorine removed herself from his proximity, blushing at what she had done, which remained ineffable.

But Daftness was smitten and now he was unable to focus on his duties. It seemed to him that his quantum soul had been hacked and the code rewritten in some mysteriously terrifying but superb manner. He strolled the perimeter fence listlessly and sighed often. He found himself wishing that Chlorine would repeat her rubbing feat exactly as before but also with variations, yet he was unable to specify to himself what form these variations should take. He was filled with an emotional nebula that was contracting slowly and eventually would form a new feeling inside, igniting under its own mass.

Meanwhile Dorc had decided to approach Yas, foster father of Chlorine, and ask for her hand in cyber-wedlock. He took platinum-plated executive toys with him as a gesture of friendship. Yas was almost tempted by the gifts to consent to giving his daughter away in marriage, but then he remembered that it was the twenty-fourth century and no female entity needed permission from any male being, nor did any male being have the power or right to make any kind of decision for female entities. That kind of thing was very archaic. So he declined to accept the toys and refused his assent regarding Chlorine, and Dorc, growling in anger, took himself home together with his newton's cradles and his perpetual motion tesseracts and musical Möbius strips.

Dorc now planned to seize Chlorine by force and waited for an opportunity to present itself. Such a chance came within a few days. A gibbering moon ape that was the pet of a visiting whirly earl escaped from a cage and wreaked havoc in the community, causing octopoids and insectoids to die of sheer fright and the local asteroid apes to turn so green with envy that half their population expired of the accelerated emerald aches, a hitherto very rare condition. But the moon ape accidentally tied itself in knots while swinging from the eaves of the galactic yoga temple and fell to the ground, where it immediately expired, and Dorc was lucky enough to stumble upon its corpse.

Nobody else was around. He used a micro blaster to skin the moon ape and when the hide was detached from the flesh, he draped it over himself. The head of the moon ape encased his own head like an ugly damp space helmet. Then he hastened to the outskirts of the chemical zone, hid behind a mutant stalagmite cluster and waited for Chlorine to pass on her rounds. But on this occasion she was not alone. She was accompanied by a vicious pack of sound hounds, sonic dogs from Sirius, and they sensed the presence of the concealed cyborg. They boomed around the stalagmites, blaring decibels at Dorc until his metal plates buckled and his flesh bits were bruised.

Ripping off the skin of the moon ape, he pressed his hands to his ears and rushed off into the distance, pursued by the sound hounds and their echoes. But Chlorine saw who they were chasing and she called them off. She still regarded Dorc as a decent hybrid of organic material and machine parts. Taking the sound hounds with her had been one of the recent ideas of Daftness, who was worried about her safety. She assumed Dorc had been playing an obscure game and that his designs, if he had any, could not be dark. Perhaps it was fashionable now for cyborgs to imitate gibbering moon apes?

And so Dorc was foiled again, for the last time too, as it happens, because a short while later something dramatic happened. Space pirates from the far side of the constellation Orion, disguised as honest traders from the near side of Taurus, entered the asteroid's interior through the spaceport crater, docked at the wharf and disgorged themselves from their craft, most dressed in photon armour and carrying antimatter scimitars. They attacked the warehouses, shops, cafes, boutiques, garages and factories, calling out exchange rates in order to preserve the illusion they were genuine merchants.

Some of them had hung weights at random positions from their clothing to alter their gait and give the impression they were robots or androids. Others had adorned themselves with fake tentacles or mandibles so that from a distance they might be mistaken for octopoids or insectoids. Many of them beeped or clanked but they made these noises with their mouths. They were rascals and villains and the sort of visitors that inhabited asteroids dread. They carried off as much stuff as they could get their gnarled hands on and what they were unable to grab with their hands they dragged behind them on long strings of solid light attached by harnesses to their photon armour.

They seized Daftness, who was rambling alone by the mineshafts, bundled him into their spaceship and started up the engines. Daftness wailed loudly and called out the name of Chlorine, who was experimenting with an augmented ear trumpet, and she heard him and understood at once what had happened. She ran to Dorc for his assistance, because he had the authority to close the crater hatch and prevent the ship from leaving, but she found him in a pool of his executive blood. He had been slashed with an antimatter scimitar and found that actually it *did* matter, rather a lot. He was expiring.

At the sight of Chlorine, reviving a little owing to the force of his love, he groaned, "I shall soon be no more, despite the fact I know many people in high places, but at least I put up a fight before I was butchered! Save your beloved Daftness, revenge me and destroy them. Listen to me carefully. As well as the normal yibban gurkles from Rumple I am also in possession of special gibban yurkles from Elpmur. Take this miniature theremin and play on it these notes that I will now whisper to you. Play them over an amplifier and leave the rest to the gibban yurkles. You will be amazed!"

Those were the last words he ever uttered. He lunged and gave Chlorine a kiss on the cheek and then his head fell back and he was no more. But she was unable to spare the time to mourn him, for there was work to do. She took the theremin and played the notes as instructed and suddenly she was surrounded by a horde of indescribable entities. They were little imps but also not at all like that. They were like an amalgam of death and custard, neutrons and mischief, a gooey fusion of spikes and quicksand. Gosh!

These were the gibban yurkles from Elpmur, the worst nightmares of the yibban gurkles from

Rumple made real. The yibban gurkles had such powerful imaginations that when they fear something intensely, they unfortunately bring it into existence. That explains the gibban yurkles to the full extent of what *can* be said about them. They are yucky and lethal and they had been trained to go berserk when the theremin played that tune.

They swarmed like festooned mamjams and took to the air on wing-things and collided with the departing spaceship, puncturing its hull with their beaks, scratching its engines into pieces with their claws, rupturing the portholes with their shrieks, and blamming the zoomers with their gortles. The way they poked the vestibules with dorsal aptitude was especially impressive. Chlorine dropped the theremin and it smashed on the ground like a humming twit. The spaceship broke open and suddenly all the pirates and Daftness were falling through the low gravity zone of the asteroid harbour.

The pirates were encumbered with their armour and weights and weapons and surliness, whereas Daftness had curled up into a foetal ball and was turning over and over. The magnus effect, which you may look up in a technical book if you like, kept him aloft and brought him gradually back to the safety of land, whereas the pirates bounced against each other and the interacting force fields of their photon armour caused explosions that wiped out most of them. The gibban yurkles picked off the few survivors, chattering as they did so, flaring their rear nostrils and sneezing like retro rockets.

This is how Daftness was saved from two perils, from the pirates and also from midair detonation, and when he uncurled and opened his eyes he saw that Chlorine was bending over him, smiling through her tears, which dripped from her plastic cheeks like rancid oil from two deflated omelettes. She told him all that had happened, explained the theremin and the tune Dorc had taught her but she neglected to mention the cheek kiss.

They decided to give Dorc a decent funeral, so they carried his corpse to the defragmenter unit, pushed it inside, wound it up and set it off. Every part of him was disassembled and rearranged according to its molecular structure. His flesh all went together in one pile, his bones in another, his metal bits in a third, his crystal and plastic and ceramic organs in a fourth, and so on. Each pile was scooped into a separate canopic jar and these were then put on a conveyor belt that would carry them to the crater crypt.

After the funeral, Chlorine led Daftness to the Garden of Galaxies, where beautiful representations of constellations and supernovae could be found down little paths. A relaxing place. Daftness felt a strange ache in his soul as he gazed at Chlorine and he wondered how this was possible because the existence of the soul had been absolutely disproved by Professor Nuts centuries earlier. He did not understand the complexities of love, that was his actual problem, because at the end of the day he was just a rustic robot.

Facet Two

It was now the middle of autumn, but in space there are no seasons, so that isn't quite true. But if they hadn't been in space then it would have been time for the harvest to begin, if they had been living in a rural environment, not in a city, but they probably would have been living in a city. Let's start the chapter again! An indeterminate amount of time had passed and Daftness and Chlorine had grown ever closer, helping each other with their work, smiling at each other, doing pleasant things and generally mooning a lot.

Mooning is considered a very respectable activity in outer space. You often see an alien or robot pulling down its trousers and aiming its buttocks, or what passes for buttocks, out of windows or portholes, and anyone who observes this phenomenon tends to regard it as auspicious and progressive. Anyway, Daftness and Chlorine were happy and kept their own trousers unbelted and down with commendable regularity and a blissful purity of motive and thus they continued in charming innocence to be companionable.

But occasionally each felt they would like to flimflam the modulus of the other with mounting passion until the partially differentiated equations of desire had to slump exhausted on the blackboards of intergalactic space, whatever that means exactly, I'm not sure. They restrained themselves, for the simple reason that neither of them knew how to flimflam. They lacked experience. Although it was a nice asteroid to live in, L35B05 was somewhat provincial and divorced from the liberal cultures of the Milky Way.

While they were mooning at a passing hover mat on which was sitting one of the sultans of swing, probably on his way to swing a deal, an old man with a fully organic heritage approached them on the broad public balcony where they were spending the evening and said, "Excuse me, my name is Philet and I have often prayed to the vacuum gods in the temple of twisting turbulence at the far end of the grotto of gunks on the obverse side of the asteroid. I have sought for you everywhere because I have something to tell you. Do you see my lips? If I purse them I look like an insane duck."

Daftness and Chlorine frowned at him in wonder, but that wasn't what he really wanted to share with them. He continued, "I own a small garden in which I grow all sorts of ancient electronic components for my own amusement. There are triodes and diodes and capacitors of all shapes and sizes and it is a pleasant place to be, if you are a historian of technology, which I am. But maybe robots and androids wouldn't care for such things, the same way I wouldn't care to see hearts, lungs and livers rising out of the soil."

Daftness and Chlorine now exchanged glances, wondering why the elderly fellow was sharing such irrelevancies with them. But he added, "As I went there today about noon I saw a peculiar being plucking potentiometers and rheostats from the branches of my resistance trees. He was a purple miniature centaur and his eyes were like spiral galaxies endlessly rotating, and when he opened wide his mouth to utter a laugh I saw that his teeth were toggle switches, some on and others off, and so I knew he was an unknown vacuum god who had come to visit my unique garden, and I prostrated myself."

Daftness and Chlorine nodded and waited for the story to continue and the old man also nodded, catching his breath, and said, "While I was spread out flat on the ground, mumbling prayers, the centaur spoke. I absorbed his wisdom and I remember every word. The workings of archaic electronic circuits are complex but can be understood with study, he told me, but the workings of destiny are far harder to comprehend. 'I am small and purple but I am older than most stars you see in the sky. I was conceived in the empty space between the very first pair of galaxies to exist. That intergalactic void was something fresh back then, and the freshness has remained with me ever since'."

"He sounds like a silly cryptic half-horse," ventured Daftness, but Chlorine nudged him in his metallic ribs with her plastic elbow, and luckily Philet, the old man, hadn't heard the remark, not that it was particularly insulting, but believers in the vacuum gods don't like it to be stated that their deities don't always make full sense. The old man was staring into the distance, as if he could peer through lost time back to his youth. He declared:

"Then I recognised this god as Dipuc, the fantastic fate manipulator, astral chemist and particle collider, he who loves nothing better than the combining of unexpected elements into new molecules. Yes, the mighty Dipuc had decided to visit old Philet in his garden of valves and semiconductors! The elements that he combines are often metaphorical or symbolic rather than physical. Hydrogen and oxygen are old hat for him, but hats and cats are something worth trying and the result might be a tabby topper. Do you see? He is powerful and strange, man and horse combined but still somehow separate."

"Is he the chief of the vacuum gods?" asked Chlorine, quite curious despite her scepticism, "Or are there higher beings in the pantheon? I get confused with the details because there are so many religions in the universe with overlapping myths. I'm sure that religious faith expresses something deep in the psychology of organic beings that can't be expressed using logic, but as an android I seem to be often befuddled by the sheer amount of divinities, deities, demigods, and other celestial beings that people like to worship."

"No, he is not the chief. The vacuum gods don't have a leader," explained Philet with a kind smile, "and that is partly because they don't exist. Lots of the gods of most religions don't exist, but the vacuum gods are aware that they don't exist, which means they are auto-atheists, and because the gods of atheists can never be overthrown (for the simple reason that atheists have no such gods) the vacuum gods are fixed in existence for eternity. They can't be overthrown even by themselves. Therefore they are the best!"

Chlorine exchanged amused glances with Daftness. "We learn something new every day. But what else did Dipuc say to you? He didn't just mutter that stuff about being older than the stars, did he? Surely there were plenty of other things he wanted to talk to you about? For instance, did he complain about his double sets of ribs? Centaurs possess two sets of ribs and that means twice the aches if you hear an extremely funny joke."

"He did not mention ribs," said Philet, "but he explained to me how gods sometimes take a special interest in particular mortals and play a game of chess with them, and he led me to believe that you two, Daftness and Chlorine, were in his magical care. For what ultimate purpose he is guiding you, it would be a gross impertinence for me to surmise. All I can state with confidence is that the great Dipuc knows who you are and is pulling the strings of chance in order to influence events that concern you both…"

The robot and android nodded at this news, slightly uneasy, excited too, a little bit sceptical also. Why would Dipuc require potentiometers and rheostats? If he didn't require them, why had he plucked them from Philet's valve garden? There were many questions but neither of them felt like trying to answer them. Daftness instead wondered aloud if he might be a god of love. "He looks like a centaur and centaurs often carried bows and arrows. Didn't the ancients believe that to fall in love was to be shot through the heart with the barbed spike on the tip of a feathered shaft? But we have no hearts."

"We do have hearts," corrected Chlorine, "but they aren't organic and they don't beat. They are notional and parabolic. Yet it is true that I feel affection for you and often dream about you. Once I dreamed that you had lost a leg and had to hop up and down to keep your balance. You kept bashing your head on a low ceiling until it was quite flat and then you were like a pillar with an unoccupied platform on top. I climbed onto that platform and stood like a statue and with an easy air of accomplishment we went bounding off into the distance. An absurd dream, true enough, but profoundly affecting."

"How strange! I also dream about you and my dreams are no less cryptic. I dreamed that you were a space melon and that I sat on you until you hatched and then you followed me around everywhere, shedding seeds that grew into other melons, until the entire asteroid was full of melons. I felt claustrophobic, so onto the surface I went, to get fresh vacuum into my metallic non-lungs but no sooner had I passed through the emergency access hatch than I realised that a giant was sitting on the asteroid, some sort of colossal robot, and that the asteroid too was a cosmic melon and was about to hatch."

Chlorine shook her head in tolerant perplexity. "One doesn't hatch melons that way. One hatches them by strumming certain chords on the uranium lute, or so I was told by Dorc. Maybe he was joking. But dreams have a logic of their own and have little to do with reality. What if Philet's encounter with Dipuc was also just a dream? He said something about an insane duck that worried me. An indirect admission of unreliability is how it seemed at the time. But no matter! It is important that we acknowledge our deepening love for each other. Maybe one day we will get to see a melon for real and find out what all the fuss is about. It would be wonderful to do that together."

"Together, you are right," agreed Daftness with a grin, "but it occurs to me that maybe we misheard Philet. He is human and old and his mouth is wonky, so it is conceivable he said *duct* instead of duck. I concede that this variation makes sense only if he was somehow hinting that he, too, is a robot. But why would he do that? And doesn't he know that robots stopped being fitted with ducts eighty years ago? We all have vents now instead."

"Unless he was just venting," said Chlorine, but they took the conversation no further and went off for a stroll and were soon cheerfully buzzed by the same hover mat they had mooned just before Philet had turned up. It was returning at a glide and yes, there was a sultan of swing sitting on it, and he shouted down to them in utter delight, "I swung that deal. I arranged for the next stellar swinging sultan conference to be held right here on L35B05. This is a great coup for me. I was in dire straits earlier but now I'm fine."

Daftness waved at him. Sultans of swing sometimes swing both ways, but there are no directions in the void of outer space, so it was impossible to deduce anything more about the fellow. He passed on, catching thermals from the heat given off by glowglobes and supernovae toads, both of which bobbed randomly along the streets as they went about their enigmatic business. Daftness watched him go and he felt wistful, he wasn't sure why, but he linked one of his arms in one of the arms of Chlorine and they went off on their stroll. It was at this point that Daftness impulsively stood on tiptoes and kissed Chlorine on her chin. He shivered with electric pleasure as he did so.

Chlorine smiled down at him and his pleasure increased to the point where he feared he might suffer a short circuit. For the remainder of the walk they said nothing to each other. Daftness might have ventured another kiss on her chin or even attempted to kiss some other part of her, and matters might have progressed with rapidity to an extremely amorous outcome, but their nascent love affair was interrupted by the following occurrence.

Some young hybrids from an adjacent asteroid known as M3THYM set off from their home in a space yacht and decided to visit neighbouring colonies for a good time. They drank the bars dry in several asteroids and space stations and finally ended up in L35B05. They dropped anchor onto the surface and swarmed down the cable and opened an emergency hatch at the base of a crater and went into the asteroid in high spirits. They enjoyed themselves in the bars and taverns and while they were getting drunk, an indigenous inhabitant of L35B05 went up on the surface and helped himself to the cable, unhitching it from the yacht, coiling it around his arm and taking it home.

This thief had broken one of his own cables and rather than buy a new one he decided it was easier just to take what was on offer. The hybrids returned to their yacht and were annoyed to see that the cable was missing. The yacht might have drifted away from the asteroid and stranded them here! They were lucky it was still where they had left it. They used their anti-gravity boots to return to the vessel and then they sailed the yacht around the asteroid to the far side, dropped an improvised cable of photons and entered through a different hatch at the base of another crater. They were still thirsty!

These hybrids of M3THYM were a motley lot. Not one of them was quite the same as any of his fellows. At this point it might be helpful to explain what a hybrid is. You know what robots and androids are. You also know what a cyborg is. Those are the three most common types of mechanical person. But there are many less common types, for example the offspring of a cyborg and an android, which is called a cydroid. Or the children of a robot and an android, which are generally known as andbots. What about the offspring of a cydroid and andbot? Well, that is called a cydbot. There are many other kinds, for example the child of a cydbot and a human is called a cydbotman, and the child of an android and an andbot is known as an andbotand, and so on. These less common types are all known as hybrids. They are marginalised.

They trooped into the first tavern they encountered, which happened to be very near to where Daftness and Chlorine lived, and they proceeded to get very drunk on a variety of strange liquids, not all of them alcoholic. While they were doing this, a mirror mouse on the surface of the asteroid happened by chance to run through the photon cable, reflecting its beam back into space, and this time the solar wind was blowing and the yacht began to move away. One of the less drunk hybrids, who had gone back onto the surface to relieve himself, saw the accident and called out for help. It was already too far away to be reached by the means of anti-gravity boots. Octopoids and insectoids hurried out through the hatch to see what the fuss was about, but they could do nothing to halt the drift of the yacht. It was sailing off on its own!

"Superconductive dented rumples!" cursed the hybrid, and he quickly went below to tell his companions the bad news. The leader of the hybrids was a powerful individual who was a roborgdroidman, which means that he was the offspring of a roborgdroid and a human being, and that the roborgdroid was the offspring of a roborg and an android, and the roborg was the offspring of a robot and a cyborg, and his physical appearance was bizarre. He had a crystal noggin that span fast on its axis without surcease, nineteen arms of different lengths and textures, one massive eye in the middle of his chest, fourteen knees on seven legs, two small mouths on retractable stalks, and boomerang-shaped feet which could fly him through the air and return him to his starting point with great fuel efficiency. His pointed ears were on the ends of his fingers.

"Somebody must be punished for this!" he bellowed, and he stomped off to find a victim, who happened to be Daftness, as he was just passing at that very moment on some errand or other. He seized the poor robot and bound his arms behind his back and was about to beat him mercilessly when Lam and Yas (do you remember them?) rushed up and insisted that, in the name of justice, there ought to be a fair trial and that Daftness should be allowed to defend himself in an official court of law. They suggested Philet as an impartial judge. The hybrids grudgingly agreed to these rational terms.

"Other terms we are inclined to agree with," boomed the hybrid leader, "are generally mathematical, in other words monomial, binomial and trinomial. Let's get this trial started and then, if we win, we will bash this bucket with a thorough attention to detail that will elicit your admiration even while it excites your deep disgust. But if we lose we shall depart, grunting and bickering and snorting, like astronomers in a treacle reactor! Oh indeed!"

Lam and Yas were joined by various bystanders and the trial began. First it was the turn of the hybrids to state their case. "We came to L35B05 in order to get drunk and ogle the females," they said, reasonably enough, "and we moored our yacht to the surface with a photon cable, because our original cable of pure osmium had been snatched by a rascal. But then a mirror mouse broke the beam of adhesive light and our yacht drifted off into the endless void. We can't accept that it was a wild mirror mouse, for no such creatures have existed for centuries. We think it was the pet of some inhabitant of this asteroid and we suspect it was the pet of this robot here, this bumblepot!"

The hybrid leader added, "As we have lost all our possessions, which were stowed in the hold of our yacht, we think it is only fair that we take this robot as part payment for our troubles. We will convey him back to M3THYM and work him as a slave until his rivets pop. A wild mirror mouse! Such nonsense! There are only domestic mirror mice and they are always kept by robots like this one. I know this for a fact because I saw it on a documentary made by the great spatial zoologist, Dorvid Clatterburra. Megapish!"

Lam and Yas nodded and conceded that the hybrids had scored some good points with their opening speech. Now it was the turn of Daftness to speak. His throat was dry and he felt unconfident and fuddled, but when he saw Chlorine in the crowd he rallied and spoke with greater animation, saying, "I never kept any sort of pet in my entire life. I have no interest in mirror mice or sound hounds or parsec cats or any other such entity. I have eyes only for the android who is my closest companion. She is the only one I wish to share my space and time with. I reject utterly that I am responsible for the drifting away of the yacht. Plus, what credence can we give to someone with an eternally rotating noggin? I also have watched documentaries and in one of them Dorvid Clatterburra said that rotary noggins are always a sign of unreliability."

The hybrid leader winced at this and flexed his flupples furiously and with agile gusto. But his chocko blocks held firm and his dingdags gully wishwashed without friction, therefore he stepped forward again and said, "Grumples to you! A rotary noggin is as beautiful as a pulsar. It whizzes and twirls with excellence. I am sure the mirror mouse was your pet."

Daftness pointed a finger at Chlorine and cried, "She is the only one I care about. Mirror mice can squeak off into the ninth dimension! I am innocent, just a robot going about his daily business, just a machine without malice aforethought or even rearward. If I wasn't made of metal I would burst into tears right now. I would flood the asteroid with salty water from my ducts. But I can't do that and the impossible must always remain undone, if the universe is to retain any sense at all. I urge the court to find me not guilty."

Philet came forward and said that he was ready to deliver his verdict. After very careful deliberation (done at high speed) he agreed that Daftness should be released. He was innocent of all charges except a fluctuating amount of electric charge and the hideous hybrids were in the wrong and ought to go away. All the bystanders cheered and applauded at this decision, but the hybrids became very annoyed and tried to seize Daftness again.

A scuffle broke out and it soon became a pitched battle. There were many hybrids but more bystanders and eventually the debauched invaders gave up and scurried away. They were chased onto the surface and they had to use their anti-gravity boots to propel themselves into space, where they bobbed aimlessly, for the yacht was too distant to catch and there was nowhere else for them to go. While they hung there, grumbling, they were picked off by a swarm of tesseract dragons that just happened to be traversing the dimensions. It was unpleasant but what can one do about such things? Daftness was free and he collapsed into the embrace of Chlorine. Lam and Yas did a strange celebratory dance while Philet played a triode like an ocarina, and the robot and the android went off together. What an incident! How exciting and odd!

But some of those tesseract dragons were compassionate beings and rather than devour the hybrids they caught up batches of them with their mobius talons and took them back to M3THYM. These hybrids summoned the other inhabitants of that asteroid and explained what had happened but they exaggerated and made it seem as if the inhabitants of L35B05 were much worse than they really were. A fleet of ten warships was assembled in order to get revenge. They landed on the surface of the asteroid, entered through the hatch, found Chlorine alone and took hold of her and carried her away. She yelled and struggled but they were strong and merciless. Daftness heard her cries and rushed to save her, but a hybrid with a neutron club knocked him brutally down.

While Daftness was in a daze, he had a sort of demented vision. Dipuc the vacuum god trotted up to him and he was chewing a star apple and he said with his mouth full of helium juice, "Don't worry about Chlorine. I am looking after her and her abductors will feel the weight of my wrath. Stay where you are and relax on the ground. That dent in your head will come to seem like the memento of a magnificent day when you look back on events. Leave everything to me. I am a vacuum god and extremely potent."

Something strange began happening to the warships on the surface. There was the sound of distant hooves that grew louder and louder and suddenly the hulls of the vessel began booming like bells. Dents appeared all over the metal bulkheads and these dents deepened and weakened the structure of the vessels. The hybrids were in a panic, vibrating in time to the boom of the hooves, thanks to resonant frequency, and they started to fall apart. An arm dropped off here, a noggin fell off there, legs and springs crumbled, chest plates shattered, and even their long antennae twisted itself into knots.

The leader of the hybrids, who had survived the tesseract dragons, ordered his followers to abandon their loot and flee on any vessel that remained intact. A slight diminishing of the hooves was heard at this point. Gyroaxis (for such was the name of the hybrid chief) was the first to seek shelter in the most undamaged craft, where he reclined on a sofa, mopped his brow with the hem of a solar sail, whistled eight dank melodies, and heaved a sigh of relief with such force that he heaved it into a nearby black hole, where it was spaghettified and mutated from the present to the pasta tense. The warships blasted away from L35B05 and they have never been seen near the asteroid again.

Daftness recovered his wits slowly and when he opened his eyes he saw the lovely face of Chlorine beaming down at him and not beaming in the sense that she was undergoing matter transmission at that juncture. No, she was smiling a radiant smile and touching Daftness on his body to soothe him. But her caresses failed to calm him, exciting him instead, and he jumped up and threw his arms about her knees and kissed the caps of those plastic joints as if they were among the most delectable hemispheres in the cosmos, akin to puddings, and they were as far as he was concerned, O besotted robot!

Facet Three

Time passed and Daftness and Chlorine grew even closer than before. Lam and Yas joked that they were going to end up fusing into one being, and even wise Philet thought that they were starting to resemble a pair of atoms bonded into a lusty molecule. But trouble wasn't entirely banished yet. Some of the inhabitants of L35B05 who tended to be more militant than the average citizen declared that the attempted invasion by the hybrids of M3THYM was insufferable and that a counter attack ought to be made. In vain were these warmongers reminded that the hybrids had failed to conquer anything.

"No matter about that detail!" cried the militants. "Our honour is at stake. It has been impugned, whatever that means, and it should be replenished. Also it must be pointed out that Gyroaxis is still alive and he is sure to be nursing a deep hatred for us. It will be safer for us to strike now and smash their asteroid before they can regroup and come back at us."

The most militant of the militants was a fellow named Chump-to-the-Three or Chump[3] and he was rumoured to have three separate brains squashed into his skull as the result of a genetic accident. He said, "Pacifism is very nice but often it is impractical and dangerous. Once I was beleaguered by a snoop. Diplomacy was useless against him. I zammed his noggin with the flupple and his shimmy deteriorated in a pulsating wobble of wave collapse. He splurged with a twimple and gokked his runtle like a microgrunt. Had I taken any other course of action, he might have done the same to me!"

Chump[3] convinced enough humans, robots, androids, octopoids, insectoids and sound hounds that he was right and war became unavoidable. His volunteer army bundled itself aboard an absorb orb and scatterwattered through space to the surface of M3THYM, where they disembarked on levitation sharks, roared through the access hatches and entered the interior of the asteroid. But Gyroaxis was already waiting for them and holding up his arms in the gesture of peace. It seemed he wanted to ask for a truce. He had watched another documentary and had learned that mirror mice *are* sometimes still found in the wild. Therefore it was essential that he offer his apologies.

Chump[3] raised his eyebrows at this news, but he was a rational being and he accepted the apology of the hybrid chief. They shook selected hands and the war was over before it had properly started. Rather unexpectedly, Chump[3] and Gyroaxis became good friends in the days that followed. Chump[3] took Gyroaxis home with him on his absorb orb. All remained sweetness and starlight between them, at least until nine grobbles had passed and they both were sucked into a wormhole while surfing the solar wind.

But let's not go off on a tangent! Peace returned to L35B05 and Daftness anticipated spending a lot of delightful time with Chlorine, but then something peculiar happened that threw their plans into disorder. There was a storm in the reality flux that vibrated the spacetime inside the asteroid, one of those very rare events that are only whispered about in the annals of doodah, and it became too hazardous to venture out of one's abode.

Daftness remained inside his pod and he was pining for Chlorine, and she remained inside her vat and thought about him. Both achingly missed the other and they prayed for the reality flux storm to dissipate, but if Dipuc (or any other vacuum god) actually heard their prayers he was reluctant or powerless to do anything about the tempest. Up and down and back and forth leapt time, space and sentience, and it made everyone nauseous until they became accustomed to it, which took a few days, like motion sickness in high gravity environments. It was very unpleasant. The reality flux storm melted some buildings and turned others inside-out and it also was responsible for opening a gateway in the fabric of causation through which something fell.

This something was a peculiar vehicle of brass, zinc, obsidian, carbon fibre and hardwood. It consisted of a frame with a saddle like a bicycle surrounded by four spinning discs that gleamed and glimmered as they turned. Perched on the saddle at the core of the device was a human being dressed in archaic clothes, a peaked cap at a rakish angle on his head and the handle of a rake stuffed down the back of his coat in order that he remain unbendingly and unendingly upright in his posture. He arrived in a blaze of viridian light and when he touched down on the ground, the reality flux storm ceased.

"Where am I?" he cried, as he blinked his big eyes behind the lenses of his academic spectacles. "This doesn't look like ancient Lesbos! Did I take a wrong turning in the chronoflow? Oh, those terrible timestreams, they are so tangled in confusion! I believe I've gone forwards into the future instead of backwards into the past. But how can I be sure? My instruments seem to have conked out. What an inconvenience for me! Ah, there is a robot over there. Maybe he will be kind enough to give me some useful information."

The robot in question was Daftness, who had ventured out of his residence the instant he felt the cessation of the vibrations of the storm. The time traveller looked at him with pleading eyes and Daftness frowned. "Why do you have that handle jammed down the back of your coat?" he asked, his curiosity proving to be more powerful than his politeness, and the time traveller explained that a stiff upright posture was essential when riding the chronoflow because to lean too far into the timestream was to risk some parts of the body ageing faster than others, to the point where they rotted and dropped off.

"That's a very good answer indeed," agreed Daftness, and he proceeded to inquire why the time traveller had chosen to visit the asteroid L35B05, but with a shrug the traveller replied, "I didn't come here deliberately, I was shunted off course by the reality flux storm. I am supposed to be going to Lesbos, an island in the Mediterranean

Sea, and researching the life story of Daphnis, a goatherd, and Chloe, a shepherdess. They are characters in a famous old story and I want to see what they were really like. My name, by the way, is Herbert Long, and I am from the year 2048 AD. I am a graduate of the University of Bromley and I am engaged in trying to finish my doctorate."

Many of these words meant nothing to Daftness, but he had taken a liking to the time traveller and he invited him to step down from the time machine and enter his home for a cup of T(ea) or C(offee) or even a cup of T(offee) which is a sticky drink that octopoids love and insectoids detest. Herbert accepted this nice invitation readily. He was sore from his journey and thirsty too and he wanted to remove the rake handle from its alignment with his spine. He dismounted with a yelp of discomfort and staggered into the supporting embrace of Daftness, who helped him into the pod where he dwelled.

The pod contained all the delights that a robot might desire, such as drills, soldering irons, screwdrivers, spanners, bows of liquid mercury, lava lamps full of real magma, boxes of long rivets, and chairs that had all their springs in good condition but no cushions to cover them. Herbert gingerly lowered himself onto one of these and achieved a queasy state of uneasy equilibrium on the wire coils and he remained there, not daring to shift his weight by so much as a millimetre. The springs groaned beneath him and he smiled stiffly while Daftness went into the kitchen to make a pot of strong T(ea).

"I want to introduce you to the woman I love but she's not really a woman, she's an android," said Daftness as he added lumps of solder to his own cup but served the beverage unadulterated to his guest. "Her name is Chlorine. She is an amazing chemical creation, the same way that I'm a stupendous metal thing. We are utterly perfect together. I am wondering if our own story might be a superior tale to that of the two lovers you mentioned."

Herbert frowned and rubbed his chin with his hand. "Your name is Daftness and the android's name is Chlorine, you say? And I was hoping to meet Daphnis and Chloe! That really is a coincidence! The reality flux storm is responsible for projecting me into the future, I have no doubt about that, but why to this asteroid and not to some other place? Now I think that the similarity of your names has a lot to do with it. Somehow the reality flux storm read my mind when I set off on my journey but it misheard my thoughts."

"Thoughts can be heard?" asked Daftness and the time traveller nodded and explained that illiterate telepaths, who can't read minds, are obliged to hear them instead, and that the reality flux storm surely belonged to that category. It clearly was illiterate at any rate, it never read any books, and Herbert knew this by pure deduction. It was a storm and storms don't read. True enough, a tornado grabs a newspaper and whirls it up in the air, flapping the pages furiously and shredding them, but that isn't the same as reading it.

"Put it this way," continued Herbert, "it could be the case that Daphnis and Chloe never actually existed. Maybe they are just fictional characters. When the reality flux storm probed my mind to discover my desire, it scanned the whole of spacetime in order to locate that pair of lovers, in order to send me to them, but the closest match it could find was you and your android. That explains why I'm here and not on some sunny blessed isle."

Daftness sipped his drink and nodded. He was a little disturbed to be told of other lovers with quite similar names who had lived thousands of years ago. It implied that time is cyclic and repeats itself, or rather that it parodies itself and he didn't care to be the actor in a parody. He took his existence very seriously. It occurred to him that if he and the android were genuine future avatars of the goatherd and shepherdess then the development of *their* tale should predict the progress of his own story. He asked in a quiet voice:

"So what happened to Daphnis and Chloe? How does the story run? I want to hear about it, if you have the time," and he stressed the word *time* to indicate that there is all the time in the universe for travellers who ride the chronoflow in an apparatus of spinning discs. Herbert was unable to refuse to tell the narrative and he began reciting a condensed version from memory. The similarities between this old yarn and events in the lives of Daftness and Chlorine were striking. Herbert saw the effect his words were having on the robot and he broke off the narrative. He said he had no wish to interfere with fate.

"I urge you to continue!" cried Daftness, "and not to pause at the point you have chosen to leave the thread of the plot hanging. There have been pirates and war, just as happened for real here, and the two young lovers were abandoned at birth, just like we were, and looked after by foster parents, as in our case, and all the other things that happened to us have been eerily prefigured in this narrative of yours! Please proceed past the point where we presently are, so that I'll learn what will happen tomorrow and the day after!

Will the android become my wife or will some disaster terminate our joy?"

"It's not right that you should be given that information," said Herbert, "as it might unbalance the universe. The future is supposed to be unclear to us. The fact of the matter is that I seem to have forgotten the ending of the tale anyway. I suppose the reality flux storm wiped it out of my memory to prevent a perilous paradox occurring. That was wise of it."

Daftness felt his entire frame droop, but he saw the good sense in what the time traveller had said. He then said that he would go and fetch Chlorine. While Herbert continued to sip from his cup, the robot left the pod and hastened to the vat where the android was floating on blended lubricants. She rose out of the vat and he blushed to see her in a state of synthetic nature. But she was so innocent that she didn't notice the effect she was having on the robot. She dressed rapidly in a proton toga and followed him. He had explained that he had a time traveller in his pod and she was excited to meet him.

Herbert stood and bowed politely when Daftness came in with Chlorine. It was immediately apparent to the time traveller that the robot and android were made for each other, not literally (for they were created for specific tasks) but in a poetic sense. He fully accepted that they were living almost the same story as their probably fictional near-namesakes, the goatherd and shepherdess, and as a result he was unable to resist whispering to the robot, "Daphnis possesses Chloe at the end. That's a detail I *do* remember," but the robot was more confused than ever and said, "Possesses?" in a faint voice.

Herbert patted him on one of his many shoulders. "Don't worry," and then he gave all his attention to Chlorine, who was gazing down at him with a smile that was shaped like a cosine wave. "Yes, my dear, I am from the 21st Century, a decade in that century in which calling female entities 'dear' has come back into fashion after a period in which it was regarded as patronising. I was planning to be whisked back to Ancient Greece but in fact I find myself inside this asteroid as the guest of a fully sentient machine. Well, we are all in the same boat and it's a boat that has a hole in it. That's my view."

Chlorine politely inquired to know more about him and his quest and so he told her most of what he could and she slowly shook her head and said, "But if we are recreating an old story and you have suddenly appeared in the middle of it and you are a character who is *aware* of how the story runs, won't that change the text in a fundamental manner? Your presence here will alter the development and outcome of the tale. It is like a feedback loop with an output that adjusts the input. You say that you went searching for two dead lovers and found us instead because we are future avatars of that couple."

"You are correct," replied Herbert, "and it could be the case that your future will now veer off at a tangent to the way it would have originally gone had I not turned up. But it might veer for only a short distance before returning to normal. It is not so easy to manipulate the future as some authorities believe. Also, I will repeat what I told Daftness here. I have forgotten almost all of the old tale and I suppose the universe erased my memory in order that I won't sabotage the plans destiny has for you. I recall only fragments."

Chlorine nodded at this and seemed satisfied with his answer and she even clapped her hands in pleasure. When Herbert had finished his drink to the dregs, Daftness suggested that he be given a tour of the asteroid. The robot and the android would be perfect guides for such an expedition, as they knew almost every square millimetre of L35B05. The time traveller agreed readily to this idea and eased himself off the uncomfortable springs and stood with relief on his own feet. Daftness said, "Come, let's start now."

The robot and the android led Herbert through the labyrinthine passages of the asteroid, through courtyards and bubbles in the stone, up stairs, down ramps, along balconies overlooking sluggish pools and rivers of liquid gases, across the wastelands of the octopoid and insectoid industrial zones. The time traveller marvelled at everything he saw and he frequently removed his academic spectacles and wiped them with a cloth before replacing them, as if he thought the lenses were tricking him in some peculiar manner.

Many of the sights were unique in the universe. Blabber gimps, anomalies of light and sound, perky plumes, kaleidoscope lakes, funfairs with rides so spectacular that other rides were irrepressibly excited to ride them and the whole thing ground to a halt as they all got in each other's way (have you ever seen a Ferris wheel riding a rollercoaster?) There was an enormous Archimedes screw in one sector that ceaselessly turned and allowed sphere imps to ascend to the surface in great quantities. They rumbled as they rolled and gleamed eerily in the luminescence of the radioactive rocks.

"Nobody knows what sphere imps are or where they come from," declared Daftness in his best imitation of an official tour guide's voice, "but we welcome them here and attempt to make their lives more bearable. They ascend for a few hours and then roll back down chutes to their starting point. They chime quietly as they do so and it's rather pleasing but also baffling. No matter! Existence has mysteries aplenty and who am I to worry that something has gone wrong if they remain unsolved? Now let us move onto the carvings of the vacuum gods in the anterior temples. These predate the discovery of the asteroid and therefore must have been sculpted by the gods themselves."

The time traveller tugged his nose at this remark. "But wouldn't that surely be regarded as self-indulgent? All beings that create religious sculptures do so of beings higher than themselves. Blizzards carve sacred sculptures of japes, japes carve sacred sculptures of men, men carve sacred sculptures of gods. It follows that gods must do the same. If these carvings were done by gods, they would be not of gods but of something higher than gods." He considered the matter for a few moments and said, "What is higher than gods? Quasars or prime numbers? Liquid helium or supernovae? I don't know."

"You are in error," responded Chlorine, "and I will explain why, but first I would like to know what blizzards and japes are? I have consulted the dictionary that is deeply embedded in my polypropylene hippocampus and it has no entries for these words. They are creatures, evidently, but of what kind I find it difficult to imagine. Clearly they were common and perhaps even rampant in your home century but have since become extinct. Doubtless we would find them as bizarre as you would find moon apes and mirror mice."

"They aren't creatures, my dear, but they are sentient nonetheless," Herbert said with a smile, "and yet for centuries they were regarded as lacking all sense and it was only in recent years (relative to the year in which I set off on my time machine) that we discovered they had minds and intelligence. Blizzards are cold storms of snow and japes are jokes played by boisterous folks. It was discovered by chance that both have individual wills and instincts, drives and motives. They are capable of deductive and empirical reasoning and this insight came as a great surprise to scientists. Blizzards sculpt japes and japes sculpt humans but their art was misinterpreted as snow drifts and pratfalls."

Daftness frowned up at Chlorine and she returned the frown. The antennae on their craniums twitched. They wondered if Herbert was mocking them and it was an unpleasant notion that this visitor, whom they had treated with kindness as an honoured guest, might be having a chuckle at their expense. But his face was set in a serious and scholarly expression and it was clear that his intentions were pure. He wished nothing more than to answer the questions put to him. Chlorine gestured at the giant sculptures around them.

"But these probably aren't religious. They might just be commemorative or done simply for decoration. True, they stand inside temples, but that isn't proof they are sacred to any faith. Indeed, it could be proposed that they are sculptures of the sculptors who sculpted those beings higher than gods you have alluded to. And the carvings of those even higher beings are invisible to our senses because we are unable to process them in any meaningful way. So you see, there is little here to annoy the logician. They are representations of the vacuum gods but they are secular in their intention and execution."

Herbert carefully inspected the monumental statues, gazing up at them and nodding his head in appreciation. He paused before one and asked, "Who is this fellow? He looks rather like a centaur," and Daftness was able to answer with an urgent note in his voice, "That is Dipuc who has great plans for us, for Chlorine and myself, I mean. He is our guardian deity, apparently, and is working to make both of us happy. For example, if you were any sort of threat he would have shot you down while you were still riding in the chronoflow. But he didn't do that, so clearly you are a positive factor in our developing equation. When that equation is solved I will be the happiest robot ever!"

The anterior temples were the last of the sights worth seeing on the asteroid and the time traveller was guided back to his machine by his new friends. It was time for Chlorine to laminate her guggles so she said a fond farewell to Daftness with a superconductive kiss and went off on her own. The robot leaned closer to the time traveller and heaved a sigh and then he said, "Please explain what you meant by hinting that I would eventually 'possess' Chlorine. It is a word I am unfamiliar with and I have no dictionary in my brain. I would be too nervous to consult one if I did, in case the word meant something unpleasant and unlucky. My sweetheart is getting her guggles coated in tetrafluoroethylene, as she does every month. While she is gone, tell me!"

"I am unable to comply with your request," sadly answered Herbert, "and it is time for me to depart and attempt to return to my own period. My mission has been a failure, yet I will remember it fondly because of your kind hospitality. Be of good cheer, that is all I can add. My worry is that I've said too much and will be punished by destiny if I endeavour to say more. Consider what you yourself told me about Dipuc and how the god would destroy me if he decided I was any kind of threat to his plans for you. Riding the chronoflow is already perilous enough. I prefer not to take unnecessary risks…"

And he refused to say more but inserted the pole of the rake down the back of his coat, mounted the saddle of his time machine, grasped the controls, pulled a lever and pushed buttons, set the surrounding discs into motion and faded with a vibrating drone. Daftness drooped and sighed, but he entered his pod and took one of the vacant seats. He wondered how he might find a way of learning what the word 'possess' means without arousing undue suspicion, then it occurred to him that arousing anything at all might be good practice for when he was alone again with Chlorine. He truly was confused.

There was a knock on the door and Daftness rose to open it. Standing there was Lynium, senior butler of Bishop Chromo. Lynium was half robot, two thirds man and one sixth experimental raccoon. He wasted no time getting to the point and said, "I overheard everything that passed between you and the odd chap who vanished into thin air just now. Religion has become a minority interest in recent centuries but I happen to know what 'possession' means and can instruct you. I have been working a long time for the Bishop! It is a spiritual phenomena. When the soul of an entity invades and takes over an individual, we say the recipient or vessel has been 'possessed'. They often froth at the mouth, twist themselves into strange shapes, pretend to be a big spider, spin their heads around on the axis of their necks and vomit lukewarm green soup."

Daftness was alarmed to hear all this, but Lynium ignored his distress and proceeded to reveal how one might possess another. The procedure involved the reversal of a ritual called exorcism, which was designed to expel a spirit that had possessed someone. If one did an exorcism backwards then he would be able to insert himself into the existence of another being and take them over. As part of his duties as an ecclesiastical butler, Lynium had access to exorcism machines. It would be easy to reverse their polarity and turn them into possession devices. He would be willing to do this for Daftness.

He went on to say that he didn't require any payment for his services, for a simple reason, namely that he, Lynium, was tired of working as a butler and had enrolled on a night school course at the local university, and had to write a thesis on theology. Using Daftness as a test subject in a reverse exorcism would help to make his research stand out from the work of the other students. Lynium wanted to be a Bishop himself one day and wear a tall comfy hat. Daftness agreed to do whatever Lynium thought best. And that was how the incident began that was to change forever the lives of the inhabitants of asteroid L35B05. It is a shame that the time traveller, Herbert Long, graduate of Bromley University, wasn't around to follow developments with his keen mind.

Facet Four

It was announced on sub-ether radio one day that the Emperor of Nine Galaxies was going to pay a visit to this system and that his tour would include L35B05 and so everyone cleaned their pods and made the interior of the asteroid as nice as possible in order to leave him with a good impression. Lam and Myr, Yas and Nubu, and Philet too, joined forces to string zinc garlands between the spires of all the dwellings and gink zarlands between the nodules of all the swellings. The spirit of communality was intensely alive.

Even Chump[3] and Gyroaxis were involved and they decorated many of the buildings by carving swirly murals into the walls with hadron blasters, whether the owners of the buildings liked swirly murals or not. By a strange coincidence the asteroid inhabitant who loathed them most fiercely was named Swirly Mural but he was sensible enough not to lodge a protest. He grinned and bore it, which was easy for him because he was a living grin that had been released from some touring hologram museum when the edges of his lips developed sores. He was a grin that spinned, but let's forget about him.

As it happened, the visit of the Emperor was incredibly brief, lasting about fifteen seconds. His spacecraft touched down, a ramp was extended, he hopped out on his mighty leg, surveyed his surroundings, turned around and went back up the ramp. Then the spacecraft blasted off and left the asteroid. He had many worlds to visit and L35B05 was too insignificant to merit more than a stopover of one quarter of a minute. Chump[3] was rather annoyed by this and wanted to immediately declare the asteroid an independent republic, but Gyroaxis helped to restrain him. Such an action would result in the instant pulverisation of the hollow space rock and every human, alien, robot, android, hybrid, octopoid and insectoid that dwelled within it. Only the vacuum gods could survive an attack from the blistering fleets of the Emperor.

Talking about vacuum gods, it was at this period that Dipuc began to show himself more often. He galloped over the roofs of buildings, used escape pods in which to perform his excretory functions, kicked over the expensive telescopes of astronomers who were studying comets and nebulae, left the seeds and pips of chewed triodes on the public walkways, shot arrows at monitor drones, kept the citizens awake at night with the sound of coconuts banging together and singing that sounded drunken but probably wasn't.

Daftness said to Chlorine one day, "Something unusual is going to happen soon and it involves me and you. I can't tell you precisely what it is, because I want it to be a surprise, and also because I don't really understand it. Tomorrow morning I will help Lynium, the Bishop's butler, with his night school work. It was something the time traveller said that has encouraged me to do this. Maybe the whole thing will go wrong and end up being a disaster. That's why I want to tell you now that you are the greatest mathematical object in the matrices of my existence and the linear algebra of my reason for being is wholly dependent on your quantity and properties. I love you."

"That's very nice," replied Chlorine, "and it almost exactly mirrors what I would say to you, had you not said it first, and when I say 'almost' I mean that the variations in our speech would be extremely minor, a question of form rather than content, minor points of grammar and suchlike. For example, I would never use the words 'unusual' or 'linear' because they leave a sour taste in my mouth, for no significant reason. I would say 'unconventional' and 'orthogonal' instead. But let's not worry about that. I wish you good luck with whatever Lynium plans for you and I hope you won't be damaged."

Daftness nodded and they spoke of other topics, and eventually it was time for him to meet the Bishop's senior butler and submit himself to the attentions of that ambitious individual. Lynium came to the pod and Daftness followed him to the Bishop's residence, a squat tower in the shape of a Klein bottle. The butler's quarters were in the upper half of the bottle. He shared them with a compressed cybermaid who was shaped like a cork but wore an apron nonetheless. She was presently away on a bob-bobbing holiday and there was no danger that Lynium would be interrupted while performing the reverse exorcism. It would be quite dangerous if there was a pause in the ritual.

"The convenient thing about living in a Klein bottle," said Lynium, "is that nobody can enter it to disturb us because it has no inside, only an outside, so it's impossible for anyone else to come in while we are here. Now make yourself as comfortable as possible. I will set up the apparatus. As you can see, it consists of the opposite of a bell, a book, and a candle, which are the items used in a normal exorcism. The opposite of a bell is a cotton sock, the opposite of a book is a long chain, and the opposite of a candle is a black sphere. You undoubtedly will want to raise an objection at this juncture and demand to know *how* they are opposites but if you think carefully you will know."

Daftness squeezed his brows together but had to admit defeat. Lynium gave him a small smile in reply, but because the robot kept frowning he finally agreed to give an explanation. "Bells resound and are hard, socks muffle and are soft. A book frees the mind, chains bind the body. Candles are cylindrical and radiate a glow, black spheres absorb light. It's very simple. Now then, the items are wired together and operate upon the victim at the same time. I recite the spell, pull the lever, and you will become a spirit. Your task is then to invade Chlorine and take over her mind, if you can manage that."

"This seems unethical to me and I'm not even sure it's what I desire," said Daftness, but then he added, "The time traveller told me it's what ought to occur in our story, so I guess I must do it. But it seems awfully peculiar! I'm a robot in love with an android and so I am required to possess her. How bizarre! Dipuc is on our side, so presumably if there is something malign in the procedure you are planning, he would intervene. Go ahead!"

Lynium now commenced the ritual, chanting and moaning, dancing a little on his raccoon feet, protruding his eyes on stalks, spinning ears like radar dishes, while Daftness sat in a chair facing the machine. This machine was a frame that contained a sock, chain and sphere connected to each other by cables. The frame started to rotate on its axis and soon became a blur. Then Lynium reached out to pull a lever and current flowed into the heart of the contraption. Daftness felt the energy bolt blast his carapace into fragments. A laser and a maser were firing in short bursts at the collection of objects inside the frame and some sort of meson masher was firing bolts of energy at the laser while a quark snacker was flossing the frequency-modulated teeth of the maser.

Daftness no longer had a body and his physicality was at an end. He was a pure spirit form, a sort of levitating presence, intangible and translucent and able to contract or expand himself to almost any size. Lynium returned the lever to its off position and blinked at the space where the robot had once sat. "You are a wandering soul now. I urge you to wander out of this building and find Chlorine and enter her through any orifice. Then you will be able to control her mind and dominate her personality. You will have 'possessed' her. That's what you wanted and that's what you will get. Cheerio!"

But no sooner had these words left the butler's mouth than Daftness entered the room at a run. How was this possible! Daftness no longer existed in material form. All the same he was here, droplets of oil running down his brow in lieu of sweat. He panted and gasped and the sound was like rusty garage doors opening and closing. He managed to shout, "Stop! Don't begin the experiment yet! This is the real me, the genuine article. Chlorine has disguised herself as me and there is a chance she will turn up here soon."

Lynium retracted his eyes on their stalks and blinked. "How can an android much taller than you possibly disguise herself as you?" He was alarmed because now he realised there had been something weird about the first Daftness, that his posture and motion were ungainly. Daftness replied, "She used a multiplicity of corsets to reduce her frame, then she squeezed into a cunning costume that was made by a craftsman. I saw his invoice when I went to visit her and found her abode empty. It was lying on the table! I knew at once what she had done. I told her I was due to meet you for an experiment, but I refused to reveal details, and I guess her curiosity compelled her to find another way of finding out the truth. It is essential that the experiment is delayed."

The butler looked at the robot sadly and shook his head. "I am sorry, but it is too late. She came here already and I thought it was you. The experiment has taken place. She has been dissolved into spirit form. She must enter a host now. That's the only way she can continue to interact with the physical universe and if she doesn't find a host soon then she may drift away and end up in intergalactic space, where it is very cold and isolated and bleak and the hydrogen clouds are so thin one can't drape them over one's shoulders like a cape, and the occasional rogue star or planet seems so out of place that the lost explorer wouldn't want to be associated with them despite the loneliness."

Daftness stared at him with the widest possible eyes. "She can possess me! I will gladly be her host," he cried, but Lynium laughed and said, "If she did that she would become a robot too and she has the soul of an android and you are in love with an android. Are you willing to be in love with a robot instead? There's very little narrative interest in two robots in love. Robot and android romance is worthy of a tale, it's the sort of thing the public loves to hear about. Even Bishop Chromo would enjoy that. But ordinary robot-on-robot passion? No, that's just run of the mill stuff. Think carefully about it."

"There's no need to think!" roared Daftness. "I am in love with Chlorine. I can't see her and I don't know where she is right now, but I will open myself to her without any conditions! She may enter me in any way she chooses and take over my mind. Let us fuse into one being inside my frame. I am a robot and she will become me, so she will be a robot too. That's fine. It is Chlorine I love, not her android identity. Come to me now, my love! Enter me and possess me! The whole of my existence belongs to you alone!"

Suddenly he grimaced and raised himself on tiptoes. Chlorine had entered him and it was something of a shock to his system. He pursed his lips, rolled his eyes and unsuccessfully fought down an urge to utter a glissando moan that went up exactly one octave. He shuddered and gibbered. Then everything settled and calmed inside him. He was a willing host and Chlorine had blended with him. It was impossible to say where one ended and the other began. Strength returned to his limbs as the innuendo-ripples of her chosen entry point into his body faded like a cheap theatrical echo. And let's be brutally honest here, robots don't have perforated rumps, so she couldn't have gone into him through that entrance, no matter how hilariously bawdy the possibility.

This should have been the end of the story of Daftness and Chlorine but the tale was told on a tetrahedral crystal (remember the Prologue?) and each facet of such a crystal must be the same size. If this facet ends here and now then it will be smaller than it ought to be and an unhappy distortion of the tetrahedron must result. Therefore more things shall happen, and they do. Lynium watched as the possessed robot left the tower that was the Bishop's residence and marched into the distance. He sighed and dismantled his reverse exorcism machine and safely stowed away the components. At least he had enough data to complete his thesis and graduate from night school. Fantastic!

The robot with the android spirit inside him decided to give themselves the gestalt name of DAFTORINE (they briefly discussed CHLORNESS as an option), never again referring to their original cognomens. They continued to walk back to the pod that had been the robot's home and now belonged to them both. While they were doing this, something extraordinary happened. It wasn't extraordinary in the sense that it was marvellous or unexpected. It was *extra ordinary*, in other words a routine occurrence, but even more routine than it should have been. It concerned a mechanic by the name of Lampy.

Lampy was human but his head resembled an incandescent lightbulb with an eerie accuracy. Because of a rare disease he had picked up while tightening nuts in Ursa Minor his skull had become transparent and his brain had started to glow. He blamed his parents for naming him Lampy because it seemed that fate had been tempted to play a punning joke on him, but the fact of the matter is that his head would have shone with a bright and steady light no matter what he was called. Other mechanics who had tightened nuts in Ursa Minor had also grown to resemble bulbs over time thanks to this disease. He was in love with Chlorine and had been (from a distance) for some time and had made up his high wattage mind to ask for one of her hands in marriage.

Today was the day he planned to plight his troth, or if that couldn't be done for some reason, then to plight some other thing of equal value, such as his sack of nuts or favourite spanner, and he was determined to press his suit so urgently that it could never be creased again, even though it was just a pair of overalls in rather a shocking condition, stained with gloop-gunk from a thousand offworld sumps and torn raggedly along its denim hems.

He had made his way to the abode of the android and knocked on the door without receiving any answer and now he was wondering what to do next. Had the time traveller not appeared in the previous chapter and diverted the narrative from its intended course, he would have played some other role in the story and perhaps ended up happy in some capacity or other, who can say for sure? But in this particular variation of the tale he was doomed. This isn't the bit that is *extra ordinary*, by the way. That bit is simply that there should exist some entity other than Daftness who fancied Chlorine and wanted her to be his. He walked away from her door with a glum expression even though his glum expressions were a darn sight brighter than most people's smiles.

At this point he turned a corner and proceeded down a narrow twisty tunnel that was poorly illuminated. Lampy was able to travel almost anywhere he liked in the asteroid because he could always see where he was going. The only places that were off limits to him were the insides of some fusion reactors, the bishop's cloakroom, the chest of pulsar drawers recovered from the wreck of a spaceship of unknown origin that had crashed millennia ago and lodged itself into the core of the asteroid, the quark cauldrons of Flamboyant Sam (who plays no part at all in this story), the canteen of insectoid workers, the casino of octopoid labourers, the domicile of the Docile Grunters of Glub, the erratic attics of any fanatic, and the unglimpsed back of the spineless beyond.

This was the same narrow twisty tunnel that DAFTORINE had decided to walk down, because its relative privacy permitted the possessed robot to smooch with itself without attracting the attention of potential mockers. DAFTORINE was doing exactly that when Lampy chanced upon them. Lampy looked and saw the body of Daftness but there was something about the way it stood that alerted him. He somehow sensed that Chlorine was present too. No longer able to resist his urges he flung himself on DAFTORINE with unsheathed lips. His passion measured more than 10,000 volt-amps at 5 volts, giving a current of 2000 amps. This was far too passionate for DAFTORINE who juddered.

The juddering had the lucky result of breaking the seal of Lampy's lips on the lips of DAFTORINE, and DAFTORINE was able to flee out of the tunnel, with the inflamed incandescent inamorato close behind. "Give me another kiss, oh you tease!" cried Lampy as he scurried along. DAFTORINE was inexperienced at long distance running and it was clear that the human would soon catch up with the poor gestalt. "Volt-amps are just a measure of apparent power," cried Lampy in an excess of lust, "and I plan to show you exactly how much true power there is in my throbbing body. In watts, my darling!"

They entered a plaza, one of the largest open spaces in L35B05 and the end of the chase seemed imminent. Daftorine was exhausted and Lampy had almost caught up. There was the song of a gong and Dipuc appeared from nowhere, his hooves striking sparks from the molecules of the recycled air. He threw back his head and neighed, even though he had a human head with a human voice, and he reached for his bow. At this point Bishop Chromo ran up, his garments flapping like the waves of a purple tsunami and his soft comfy hat wobbling on his head. He was livid with indignation. "Sacrilege! Someone has been conducting horrid reverse exorcism experiments in my house!"

He paused as he saw Daftorine on the other side of the plaza. He pointed at them with a fat finger. "I believe you know something about this heresy!" and he would have said more, but Dipuc reached down and picked him up, nocked him like an arrow to his bow, drew the string back, took aim and loosed him straight at Lampy. The bishop collided with the mutated electro-man and both splattered in a shower of ecclesiastical blubber and libidinous glass fragments. Dipuc gave a curt nod to Daftorine and then popped back into the vacuum that was both his home and his substance. Truly, as Philet had intuited, he was the guardian of the perfect love embodied in the gestalt's frame.

The tale is done, the adventure is over, doubtless everybody lived happily ever after, unless they didn't, and yes, we must blame the time traveller for the inconvenient fact that this futuristic retelling of the ancient story of Daphnis and Chloe went off in a new direction and kept going that way. As a brief aside, the defeat of Lampy by Bishop Chromo was witnessed by Chump[3] and Gyroaxis, who were very impressed with what they saw. They decided to shoot each other from bows too, just for their own pleasure.

When Gyroaxis first suggested the idea to Chump[3] he received the advice that, "Such a game might dent your noggin," to which the hybrid retorted, "My noggin was dented long ago, when your great-great-great-great-great-great-great-great-grandfather's nappies were still growing in the cotton fields of Arkansas on Old Earth. Shoot me at a target or our friendship is over! Make that target a very ripe melon of colossal girth!" How could Chump[3] continue to protest in the teeth of such a persuasive speech? Well, he didn't.

A tetrahedron has four equal sides. The holograms on the four facets of the crystal that I viewed in the museum were not quite of equal size. How could this be? I turned and asked the curator how a tetrahedron that looks perfectly formed could in fact be distorted. He answered me as follows, "The crystal really is an absolutely regular tetrahedron. But in your literary rendering of the holograms, there is a discrepancy of scale. The wordage of your first facet is approximately 3786, but of your second facet is 4280, and of your third is 4416. The meaning of this is that you are approaching the crystal. That is why the facets seem to be growing bigger. It's a trick of perspective."

I was surprised by this, because it didn't seem to me that I was moving at all, but the curator explained that the floor of the museum was made of Teflon. I was sliding towards the crystal without realising it. The floor of the museum lay on a shallow gradient. If I didn't take evasive action I would eventually hit the crystal and the holograms would discharge themselves into me, destroying my brain. I heeded his warning. With a great wrenching of my entire body, an awful contortion that pained my skeleton, I pulled myself away from the crystal. The facet I was viewing, namely this one, became smaller as a consequence, and in fact is only 3671 words long. I am safe again.

THE END

This book
isn't really dedicated
to Evolution and Mutation
but to my wife,
Maithreyi